The Yellow Aeroplane

William Mayne was born in England and educated at the Choir School in Canterbury. His first book was published in 1953 and since then he has written numerous books for children. In 1957 he was awarded the Carnegie Medal for his book *The Grass Rope* and he has been commended for this award ten years running.

William Mayne

The Yellow Aeroplane

illustrations by Trevor Stubley

Piccolo
Pan Books London and Sydney

First published in Great Britain 1968 by Hamish Hamilton Ltd
This edition published 1979 by Pan Books Ltd,
Cavaye Place, London SW10 9PG
© William Mayne 1968
Illustrations © Trevor Stubley 1968
ISBN 0 330 25615 7
Printed and bound in Great Britain by
Richard Clay (The Chaucer Press) Ltd, Bungay, Suffolk

one

'I'll do it all,' said Rodney, holding out his hand for some money. Mother felt in the silky inside of her handbag and brought out a scented pound note. It had taken the smell from the bag. New notes smell like roast beef.

'Half single,' said Mother. 'Grandfather will pay for you to come back.'

Rodney went to the ticket office and looked in through the hole in the glass. A man looked down at him.

'You're supposed to talk through the hole up here,' said the man, pointing to another place where the glass was cut away.

'I can only reach that with my fingers,' said Rodney, touching it. The speaking hole was much too high, unless someone lifted him up.

'I can hear you just as well from down there,' said the man. 'What would you like?'

'A half single,' said Rodney.

'That should be easy enough,' said the man. 'Where do you want to go? You'll have to tell me.'

'My grandfather's house at Kenge Common,' said Rodney.

The man pulled a ticket out from a place in the wall, put it into a machine that made a bumping noise, and then handed it to Rodney. 'That'll take you as far as Kenge Station,' he said. 'That's as far as the railway goes. You know, it doesn't go right to anybody's house.'

The ticket was green, with black writing. It had hard corners. Rodney said thank you for it, and brought it back to Mother. Then the man called him again, and gave him a handful of change. Mother poured all the coins into her bag, and then weighed it in her hand to show how much heavier it had become.

They went on to the platform to wait for the train. Rodney was carrying the ticket carefully, because he did not want to bend it. But the man at the little gate to the platform put out his hand, took the perfect ticket from

Rodney, snipped a piece out with his things like pliers, and gave it back.

'I've just bought that,' said Rodney, looking at it. 'And you've spoiled it.'

'I have to,' said the man. 'I spoil them all.' But he very kindly bent down and looked on the ground, and picked up the piece he had cut out, and gave it back to Rodney. 'There,' he said. 'Put it together in the train. It'll give you something to do.'

The train came in, and stood there with its diesel engines beating. Doors clanked open and banged shut. Mother pushed him to one of the doors while it was still open, and he stepped up into the train. Mother put his little case inside the door.

'There,' she said, 'there's plenty of room to sit down. Don't forget to get out of the train at Kenge. Give everybody's love to Grandfather and Granny.'

'And be a good boy,' said Rodney. 'Mother, you be a good girl.'

'I will,' said Mother, and she stood up tall, and Rodney bent low, and they just managed to give each other a kiss through the train window. Then the engines roared, and the train began to leave the station. Mother stood away from the train. Rodney watched her. There was still time, he thought, for her to open a door, and jump in, and come with him. And then there was no time for that, because the train was going too fast. But there was still time to stop, and Mother could catch up. Then it was too late for that, because the train had left the station and was among the houses.

Rodney picked up his case and found a seat. He put the case on the seat beside him, and looked out of the window. Then he looked at the ticket, with its chopped-out piece. He put the piece in its place, and the ticket looked right again. Then the piece fell out, and he put both parts in his pocket.

The train stopped at a station. He went to the window again and looked out. Mother could have come very quickly to this station and got on here. But there was no one on the platform but a railway man. The train waited a moment, and then left. Rodney sat down again.

At the next station he looked out again, but there was still no Mother. But he really knew she would not be there. And at the third station he forgot to look at the platform at all. The only thing he did was read the name of the station on the platform the other side, to see that it was not Kenge. It wasn't.

The train went on through the town, where it was all houses. Then it left the town and came among villages. And Rodney found, once, that he could not see any houses at all from the window. There was nothing but fields, and a little wood, and hills in the distance.

Kenge was among the hills. The train began to get into cuttings, where the ground had been nipped out like the nipped-out piece of ticket, in a V shape. The sides of the V went higher. A bridge sped by overhead, and then another, and then a tunnel closed in over the train, and all the yellow lamps came on in the carriage, and it was noisy.

Then the train squeezed out of the tunnel and was among trees, and then it was at Kenge station.

Grandfather was on the platform, looking into every carriage as it came by. He came to Rodney's door and opened it, and that was a good thing, because there was no door handle inside at all. Rodney was glad he had not noticed before, or he would have worried all the way to Kenge. Even now he could still worry a bit about what would have happened if Grandfather hadn't been there.

Grandfather took the little case. 'We'll just watch the train go out,' he said. 'Then we'll go.'

Rodney found his ticket. He wondered whether he had to give both pieces up, or whether some more would be cut away from it, and he would be able to keep it.

The train went out, and round a curve, and out of sight in the trees of Kenge Common. There was quiet when it had gone.

'Well, how are you?' said Grandfather putting his arm round Rodney and squeezing a bit, to show he was pleased to see him. Rodney put an arm round Grandfather and squeezed back, but his arm did not go very far round, and it was not much of a squeeze.

The man at the barrier took both pieces of ticket,

looked at them, fitted them together, and gave back the little piece. 'I don't want it all,' he said.

'He's kept the best piece,' said Rodney; and they began to walk to Grandfather's house.

two

Granny and Grandfather lived in a house that was exactly like the one at home, except for the furniture and the wallpaper. The kitchen sink was the same, the gas cooker was the same, the fireplace in the sitting-room was the same, and the garden gate made the same squeak and click. Grandfather said it was because both houses were Council houses, and they must have been built from the same plans.

Granny heard the garden gate, and looked from the window. Rodney thought it was like coming home, because Mother would hear the gate at home and look from the window in the same way. And Granny was just like Mother.

It seemed that the whole family was like each other, because Granny, when she had kissed him, said, 'You get more like your Grandfather every day, Rodney. Or perhaps your Grandfather gets more like you. He gets naughtier, though.'

'I get gooder,' said Rodney. 'And they all send their love.'

'Good,' said Granny. 'And now let's have our dinner.'

The dinner was made special by having pop served with it. Granny's first dinners were always special. The pop fizzed in the back of Rodney's throat, and Grandfather patted him on the back, and Rodney hiccupped.

'Now, you two,' said Granny. 'Let's have good manners from you as well, Grandfather.'

Rodney drank the rest of the pop with great care, squeezing the fizz out with his tongue before swallowing.

After dinner Granny washed up, and Grandfather sat in his chair and lit his pipe, and then went to sleep. Rodney went into the garden at the back of the house. It was a very different garden from the one at home. The houses were the same; but this garden went a long way back, uphill at first, and then flat, and instead of having another garden beyond it at the end, there was a wood. The wood was on a hill, and went up and up.

Rodney went right to the end and leaned on the fence. Behind him he could see only the bedroom windows of the house. In front was the quiet woodland full of standing trees and shadows.

He listened. There was no noise of traffic, no noise of children playing, no noise of radios. At first there seemed to be no noise at all. Then he heard the country-side talking to itself. There were bees among the flowers of the garden, humming to themselves. There was a dog in the distance, shouting to a friend. There were birds in the trees, singing and flying and murmuring. There was one quite near, and he heard its wings flutter against the air like a book being shaken.

Grandfather finished his sleep and came into the garden, lighting his pipe again. It had not burnt very far before he fell asleep after dinner. He buried his match in the edge of a flowerbed, and looked round the garden to see what he should do next. Rodney was glad to see him, because he had begun to feel he was alone, with only animals making noises round him, and not saying anything he could understand.

Grandfather decided to trim the edge of his lawn. Rodney said he would pick up the grass as it was cut. Grandfather crawled round the edge with the shears and snipped, and Rodney crawled after him with a basket and gathered up the grass.

They did the little lawn, and then went round the lilac bushes to the big lawn. Grandfather clipped faster than Rodney gathered, so that he was round the corner first. Grandfather did not see what happened next.

Rodney was pressing a handful of grass down into the basket, feeling the cool blades and smelling the cut edges, when there was a noise above him. It was a very little noise, hardly more than the noise of a small breeze rustling the trees. But there was a shadow too. The shadow went across Rodney's hand and arm, and he looked up.

There was an aeroplane in the garden, flying round in a circle. It had flown over Rodney's head and touched the leaves of the lilac. Now it was flying lower and lower, and

coming towards him again. If he stayed where he was, it would hit him on the head with one of its wings. He stepped aside, and the aeroplane went by again, and then landed itself in the middle of the small lawn, and stood still.

It was a big model. Its wings were two feet across, and painted in black and yellow stripes, like a wasp. It had a propeller, but it was not going round now. The aeroplane sat in the grass. Rodney watched it. He thought it might start up again, and take off. But nothing happened.

Round the corner Grandfather clipped on. He stopped once and lit a match, and then he went on. Rodney watched the aeroplane. He had a feeling that, since it had landed so cleverly, there might be very small people in it, and that in a moment they would get out, and ask where they were.

No one got out. Nothing happened. Rodney walked a little closer. Then he thought that an aeroplane is not a wild animal, and he went right up to it, bent down, and picked it up.

It was very light. It was like picking up a leaf. It was made like a leaf, too, like a dry autumn leaf. There were hard parts, like veins, and he could feel them, and there were stretched parts between, where there was a papery skin, so tightly fixed on that the hard parts had sunk in a little. He tapped the papery skin on one of the wings, between the ribs, and it made a hollow noise.

There was a part of the aeroplane that was unpainted, underneath its body. All the rest was black and yellow, but this piece was nearly clear. Inside there was the rubber that made the propeller go round. Now it was slack and soft. Rodney turned the propeller a little, and the rubber inside turned with it and began to tighten up.

He let go of the propeller, and it turned round twice, though he had wound it ten times. But it was enough to show that was how it worked.

Grandfather's clipping came nearer and nearer. Grandfather himself came round by the lilac tree again. 'Well,' he said, 'mind you don't break the windows with that.'

'I didn't bring it,' said Rodney. 'It flew into the garden and landed on the lawn. It was a perfect landing.'

'Someone will be round for it in a minute,' said Grandfather. 'So be careful with it.'

Rodney put the model down on the grass again, and looked at it. It looked like a real aeroplane in a big field. Rodney let his eyes be in another aeroplane high up in the air, looking down.

'I'll finish your job for you if you like,' said Grandfather.

'Oh, no,' said Rodney. 'Mother says I have got to be helpful.'

three

Rodney filled the basket with grass clippings twice, and
went to the end of the garden and put them on the heap
where all the grass clippings, and tea leaves, and leaves
from the trees were always put. He sprinkled the leaves
on the heap, and then pressed his fingers into the grass
that was already there. It was soft and warm and rich-
smelling. He pressed his fingers in deeper and the warm
turned to hot, and the softness turned to a sort of wetness,
and the smell grew richer and stronger.

When the edge of the grass was clipped Grandfather
mowed the middle of it. Rodney took up the aeroplane,
which would have been in the way, and took it down to
the house.

'Have you just made that?' said Granny. 'You never
had that in your little case when you came.'

'It isn't mine,' said Rodney. 'It just landed in the garden, on the grass. And nobody got out.'

'They wouldn't have,' said Granny, looking at the aeroplane. 'There aren't any doors.'

'There aren't any people,' said Rodney.

'Don't you know who it belongs to?' said Granny.
'Doesn't your grandfather know?'

'He said somebody would be coming for it,' said
Rodney. 'But no one has.' He hoped Granny would say
that he could keep it himself; but she said that it still
belonged to someone, and the best thing to do was to wait
for the rest of the day, and see whether someone did call
for it, and then, if no one came, the aeroplane should go
to the police station.

'Oh,' said Rodney, and he put the aeroplane on the
table, because he knew he couldn't have it, and he didn't
want to get used to it. He thought he had better stop
touching it.

'And then, you see, if no one asks for it for two months,
then you can keep it,' said Granny. 'I think that's the
rule.'

'Two months,' said Rodney. 'That's a long time.'

'It is and it isn't,' said Granny. 'Stop thinking about it, and after tea we'll go down and see what the policeman says. And now go out and help your grandfather.' Granny looked from the window to see where Grandfather was, but he was not in sight in the back garden. She looked out at the front garden, and opened the window. Rodney thought she had seen Grandfather, but she shouted out: 'Maureen Garley, stop swinging on that front gate and go away. Be off with you.' Then the window was closed with a bang. Rodney stroked the aeroplane, just behind its wing. If it felt things, he thought, it would like that.

'The way some children are brought up,' said Granny. 'I don't know what's to become of us, or of them.'

'I think I'll go out in the garden again,' said Rodney.

He was out in time to carry the grass box to the end of the garden and tip another layer on to the heap. This time he stood there so long laying the fresh cool green cuttings out level that Grandfather came for the box and took it back himself, and left Rodney to play. 'You'll never make a gardener's boy,' he said. 'Unless they put you to work in a dream garden.'

Rodney thought that was true. He had been levelling the grass to make aerodromes where black and yellow aeroplanes could land. He finished one layer of greenness, and imagined the aeroplane taking off from it. It circled overhead, he thought, and then went off on some dangerous journey over the fence, among the trees of the wood.

There was somebody in the wood. Rodney knew that people could go in the wood as much as they liked, because it was common land, and belonged to everybody that lived in Kenge. No cars were allowed in, though. Cats that had gone wild lived there, and goats, and some cows, and there were squirrels everywhere. Squirrels used to come into Granny's house and steal food.

It was not squirrels or cows or cats, or even goats, that Rodney saw. It was two boys, and they were stalking somebody, a third person that Rodney could hardly see. He forgot the aeroplane, and he forgot the grass, and he forgot that he should not climb the fence. He put

one foot on the edge of the compost heap, the other on the top of the fence, and jumped down into the grassy edge of the wood, and crouched there. Then he began to stalk the stalkers.

It was easy to do. They made a lot of noise. Rodney thought he was making much less. At first he crawled in the grass under the trees, and then he crawled in bracken and then he crawled among tall stuff that was under the trees. Then he gave up crawling, because the ground was bare ground and it was stony. He was among the tall stems of elder and hazel, and he could hardly see where he was going.

He stood up and followed the noise. Then the noise stopped, and there was perfect quiet in the wood. There was no sound at all, not even a bird. Then flies began to buzz, and to gather round his head. He was hot, and the flies tickled him, because they kept landing on him. He stood in the middle of the bushes and slapped his own face; but it made no difference to the flies.

He walked on a little way, and came to a big tree, an oak, standing by itself in a little clearing. He stood under it and listened. There was nothing to hear. Everything was quiet.

Something bigger than a fly came past his face and landed in the grass, and lay there. He bent down to pick it up. It was an acorn, a very old, dry, yellow one. It had fallen from the tree.

Something else came down. This time it hit him on the head, and bounced away. He rubbed his head, just behind his ear, and picked up the thing that had fallen. It was a little shiny stone.

Stones do not grow in oak trees. Rodney turned round and looked up. He did not know what he would see. He looked up without thinking about it, because it was natural to look and see where falling stones came from.

He saw the big branches of the oak tree. He saw the thousands of leaves, and the sky beyond.

He saw a little house high in the branches of the tree, and he heard someone move in the little house. Whoever it was had moved because he had looked up.

He looked for a way to climb the tree. If people drop

things on your head from a house in a tree, that is rather like an invitation to climb the tree and visit them. If people don't want you, they should take no notice.

There did not seem to be any way up the tree at all. There was a wide trunk with its deeply carved bark. But there were no branches to take hold of for a long way. Rodney thought that if he had been twice the height he would not have been able to reach one.

four

It was very quiet, up in the house in the tree. No one made a sound, no one dropped things down.

It was not so quiet at the bottom of the tree, where Rodney was. He meant to be quiet, but he made more noise than he wanted. He was trying to climb the tree. The branches were too high to reach, so he tried to cling to the bark and get up that way. He clung with his fingers, and lodged his toes in cracks and crevices, and pushed and pulled. He could get so far, and then he would fall off the tree, and land with a thud. Once he landed on his back. The tree did not help him at all.

Then there was a noise high in the tree. A door opened and shut. Leaves began to rustle, and small branches began to move. Rodney stopped struggling to climb things that did not want to be climbed, and looked up.

Some dustiness from the tree came down and got into his eyes, so that they watered as if they had been in a strong wind. But he saw a boy climb down among the branches, and stand overhead, looking down at him.

'I'm not crying,' said Rodney, rubbing his eyes.

The boy said nothing. He walked along the branch above Rodney's head, away from the trunk, until the branch was almost too thin to hold him. The branch bent towards the ground, and the boy came with it, because it was his weight that made it bend. Then he jumped on to the ground.

'How did you get up?' said Rodney.

'Secret,' said the boy.

'Tell me,' said Rodney.

'One day,' said the boy. 'What's your name?'

Rodney told him. The boy's name was Leo, he said, but Rodney did not know whether that was true, because the boy had to think before he said his name. Rodney asked the names of the others. Leo looked at him and said, 'What others?'

'I saw you,' said Rodney. 'You were with another boy,

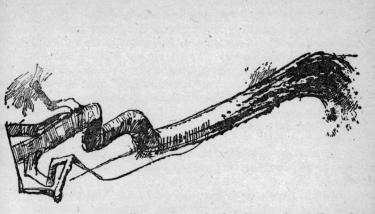

and you were following somebody else, and I followed you, and then you weren't there any more, but up in the tree, in that house.'

'It's a Nest,' said Leo. 'We live there. We're the Three Bad Eggs. We're pirates, and things like that. Me and Northman, and Armadine.'

'I've forgotten your name,' said Rodney, though it was not true at all.

'So have I,' said the boy, when he had thought. 'What did I say it was?'

'Leo,' said Rodney. 'And Northman and Armadine.'

'And there's another one,' said Leo. 'But she doesn't have a name yet.'

A shower of shrivelled acorns came dropping through the leaves of the oak tree, and scattered themselves over Rodney and the boy who called himself Leo. There was a sort of hissing whistle from above, and somebody said, 'It's her,' and Leo said, 'We have to go away now, quick.'

He pushed Rodney away from the tree. They both went in among the thick small bushes at the edge of the clearing, and then crawled out beyond into the bracken, and waited at the edge of it.

'There she is,' said Leo. 'That's the biggest enemy.'

There was a girl walking in the grass beyond the bracken. She was following a path, and looking round her carefully.

'Do you have girls for enemies?' said Rodney.

'We don't want to bother with her,' said Leo. 'She makes herself into our enemy. She keeps finding us. But she hasn't found us yet. She's Maureen Garley, and she always wants to be in everything, and we are sick of her.'

'She was swinging on my granny's gate,' said Rodney. 'But I didn't see her. She told her to go away.'

'She's always saying things like that,' said Leo. 'She hasn't got very good manners. And she copies at school without asking.'

'It was my granny that told Maureen Garley to go away,' said Rodney. 'My granny doesn't go to school any more.'

'I didn't mean your granny,' said Leo. 'And now let's talk very loudly and walk away from the Nest and Maureen will follow us. Just pretend you are a Bad Egg, and she won't know the difference. Think of being a pirate or a bandit, and you'll look like a Bad Egg.'

Rodney tried to look like a Bad Egg, and walked along with Leo, through the grass and down to the fence behind the gardens of the houses.

'My grandfather lives along here,' said Rodney. 'It's this garden here, that we've got to now.'

He could see Grandfather in the garden, and heard him call, 'Rodney, tea-time.'

'You'll have to go,' said Leo.

'I'll have to go,' said Rodney.

'I'll lead her away,' said Leo. Maureen Garley had been following, stalking from bush to bush, and hiding behind trees that were much too thin to disguise her at all. Leo gave Rodney a push up over the fence, and Rodney jumped down into the garden.

'Now,' said Grandfather, 'if we were meant to cross that fence it would have a gate in it. If you want to be on the common you have to go round by the road.'

Rodney looked round at the fence. Somebody looked over it.

'You see,' said Grandfather. 'You'll have Maureen Garley over it before long, and we don't want that.'

After tea Granny thought she wanted to be rid of the aeroplane, because it was too big for the house, and no one had come for it at all. 'I think we'll take it to the police station,' she said. 'That's where people will ask about it. And then they will tell us whether it has been claimed.'

Granny put on a cardigan, and picked up her handbag. 'You carry the aeroplane,' she said to Rodney. 'You'll have to come, because you found it.'

Rodney was glad to be carrying the aeroplane through

the village of Kenge. It was very nearly like owning it, he thought. People might think he had made it, too. He thought he could make one like it, if he had the wood and the paper.

Then, as he was thinking things like that, he saw someone standing in front of him and Granny. It was Maureen Garley. He thought she looked rather big and strong.

'Here,' she said, putting out her hand and touching the aeroplane. 'I saw that first. I must have done.'

'Go away, Maureen Garley,' said Granny, and she snatched the aeroplane from Rodney, held it high over her head, and walked on towards the police station. Maureen Garley stood on tiptoe for a moment, but she did not grab the aeroplane. She looked very angry, and walked away, muttering to herself. Granny walked on with the aeroplane overhead still, as if she were playing flying.

five

The policeman looked at the aeroplane. He said there might be a name written on it, but he could not find it. Granny said she had looked. Then he wrote down in a book Rodney's name and Granny's name, and gave the aeroplane back. 'We don't want that down here,' he said. 'There isn't room for it. You'd better take it back home, and if I get any inquiries I'll send them on to you.'

'Is it mine?' said Rodney. 'Is it mine now?' But the policeman shook his head.

'I'll let you know,' he said. 'I shouldn't let him play with it,' he said to Granny.

'It's not him I'm worried about,' said Granny. 'It's that noisy little Maureen Garley. You'd better send her away, or we shan't get this aeroplane home.'

'I expect you'll be able to manage,' said the policeman. 'She won't go away if I tell her.'

Maureen Garley was outside. 'What have you been telling him?' she said, standing in front of Granny. 'And you can't have that model, boy. I saw it before you.'

Granny thought she had had enough of Maureen Garley. She reached out her hard hand suddenly and slapped her on the seat of her jeans, and said, 'That's enough from you.'

Maureen Garley thought it was enough from Granny, too. She walked away, not muttering this time. Granny walked on, swinging the aeroplane and still looking rather cross. Rodney walked behind, until Granny turned round and snapped at him. 'Don't trail along,' she said. 'Come and walk beside me. Where are your manners?'

She was in a good temper by the time they were home again, and she said she was sorry for turning on Rodney. Rodney thought she was not very different from Mother: they both had their biting times. The aeroplane went on top of Granny's wardrobe, sharing the space with a furry hat and a pair of boots. Granny said it would have to

be dusted, but otherwise it would be no trouble. Then Rodney had supper and went to bed.

In the morning he woke up and looked out of the window, to see which house he was in. He saw the garden and the woodland beyond, and heard only the quiet of the countryside, and knew he was at Kenge, and not in the town.

After breakfast he went for a walk with Grandfather. That was a thing that happened every day at Kenge. They went on to the common, going round by the road to get in, and walked along the edge to the next way in, called at the shop for a paper, and came home again. Then Grandfather read the paper. Rodney went out again.

He thought he would climb the tree to the tree house, the nest where the Three Bad Eggs lived. He knew he shouldn't do so, but he climbed the garden fence, because it was the quickest way. Then he searched about until he found the tree. No one dropped anything on him today. He looked up and he listened, and then he tried to climb the trunk again.

It was no good. He could not cling on long enough to get to a branch. He even tried taking his shoes and socks off and clinging with his toes; but that only made his feet hurt. Then he thought of the way that Leo had walked along a branch and come down to the ground that way. He followed the branch along.

He saw something tied to the branch. A rope was looped on to it, and one end hung down a little way. Rodney thought that if he took a running jump at the rope he might get hold of it and swing himself on to the branch. He took several jumps first, but he did not quite get to it. He stepped back, and ran and jumped. At the third jump he caught hold. He pulled with his arm, and tried to swing upwards. But the rope gave way in his hand, and came loose. Instead of finding himself hanging from a rope and in the air, he found himself lying on a lumpy tree root, with the rope on top of him.

But it was still fixed to the branch above, and it was a rope with knots in it. He pulled it to make sure it was still firm, and began to climb it. It swung about as if it wanted to knock him off, but he held on. And then his arms were on the branch, and after his arms one leg, and then the other, and he was sitting on the branch and the leaves were rustling and rattling all round him, and the rope swinging below and bending the grass. He pulled the rope up after him, and laid it on the branch, just as it had been. Then he

stood up, and walked perfectly easily to the trunk of the tree, and then up on to the next branch, and the next, like a staircase, until he came to the little house.

It was made of wood. It had a locked door, and a fastened window, an iron roof painted black, and a chimney with a hat on. On the door it said: 'The Nest. The Three Bad Eggs. Private Nest. Maureen Garley go away.'

Rodney knocked on the door. There was no reply. But there was a noise from somewhere. Rodney held on to the door with two hands and looked down to the ground. It seemed a long way. There was somebody down there, looking up towards him. It was Maureen Garley.

He kept still. Maureen looked all round, and seemed to think no one could see her. She pulled something from her pocket, a small thing, and held it in her hand. Then she put it against the trunk of the tree and held it there. Rodney did not know what she could be doing, until she bent down and picked up a hammer, and started to knock the nail, which is what it was, into the tree.

The tree did not notice. Rodney thought it would shake, but Maureen was not hitting hard enough. She knocked one nail in, and then put another a little higher, and a third above that. She put the hammer down and began to climb the tree, using the nails as a ladder.

Rodney wondered what he should do. But he did not have to do anything. Maureen got on to the first nail with one foot, and on to the second with the other. Then she fell off the tree, and landed on the ground. She lay there and muttered, and got up again. The two nails had fallen out of the tree when she put her weight on them. She tried to hammer them in again, but they would not go in far enough. One of them bent itself over, and the next one suddenly sprang away from the hammer, and she could not find it, because it went among the roots and grass.

Then she listened, and took her hammer, and crept away. She went out of sight. A moment later Leo appeared, and two others with him. They had a stick with them, and they were about to reach up to the end of the branch for the rope. Rodney knew that Maureen was watching, and would find out how to climb the tree.

'Maureen Garley's watching,' he shouted. 'Don't come up.'

six

The Three Bad Eggs stood still. For a moment they looked up towards Rodney. Then they went to the edges of the clearing where the oak tree stood, and looked out among the trees. But it was Rodney who saw Maureen Garley. She was running away. When she was halfway to the fence at the back of the houses she turned round and shouted something, and then ran on.

'She's gone,' said Rodney. And he wondered what the Three Bad Eggs would say to him, now that he was at their Nest.

They all came up, in exactly the way he had come, except that they did not jump up to find the end of the rope. They did it an easier way, by pulling it down with a stick. They came and stood beside Rodney, all on branches.

'Hullo, Leo,' said Rodney, when they were all there.

'Oh,' said Leo. 'That's me, isn't it.'

'Usually David,' said another Bad Egg, a girl. 'He makes these things up and then he forgets them. What's my name, Leo?'

'I've forgotten,' said Leo. 'Armadine, I expect.'

'That's what you said yesterday,' said Rodney. 'And there was Northman.'

'That's John,' said Armadine. 'And I'm Susan. We haven't brought the other one. She can't climb up things.'

Rodney wondered what they would say to him about being up here without really being invited. Leo looked at him, and said: 'You've got here, so you might as well stay. It's that Maureen we won't have.'

'She hurts us,' said Armadine. 'She twisted John, I mean Northman, dreadfully once, and he wouldn't come right.'

Northman grunted, and then twiddled his fingers, which meant that he wanted the key of the Nest. Armadine gave it to him, and he opened the door and went inside, without saying anything more.

There was hardly room for four of them in the Nest.

They could not stand up, except for Northman, who could stand by one wall where the roof was higher. The rest of them had to kneel.

'We sometimes bring our dinners,' said Leo. 'But sometimes we don't stay very long.'

'There's a reason,' said Armadine. 'But we don't know what it is.'

Rodney said it might be Maureen Garley; but they said that it couldn't be her. It was a noise, they said, and a sort of somethingness, and they hoped it wouldn't come today. They did not say what sort of noise it was, or what it did. Rodney wished they would, so that he would know what to expect.

They stayed in the tree for the rest of the morning. Leo took Rodney right up to the top, to where the branches were thin and wavy, and where he could see over the hilly top of the common one way and over the village the other, into the gardens and closes and places he could not see from the road. He saw Grandfather in the garden, bent over a flowerbed, weeding.

Leo pointed out the house where the Bad Eggs lived but Rodney was not sure which one he meant, in the end. He showed Rodney Maureen Garley's house, and there was Maureen on the fence, talking to people who went by.

'She's just cheeking them,' said Leo.

They went down from the tree-top to the Nest again. Leo had a watch, and he looked at it, and was beginning to say that it was time they went home, when the tree trembled. It had not trembled when Maureen Garley drove nails into it. But now it shook, and the roof of the Nest shook as well.

'That's the somethingness,' said Armadine. 'Let's go down before the noise.'

But they were still up there when the noise came. It was a roaring noise, not very loud, but very deep, and going on for a long time. It came from somewhere deeper in the common, where the woods were thicker. After it there was quiet. They climbed down the tree quietly, and stood together at the bottom of it, and looked at each other.

'Leo thinks it's a dragon,' said Armadine. 'Or a wolf.'

Northman grunted in agreement. Leo said they had to go home anyway, so it didn't matter what he thought.

They walked together to the edge of the common, where the road was, and the proper way on and off.

'You must come again,' said Leo; and Armadine nodded her head to show that she agreed. Northman looked at him in a friendly way. Rodney knew that they really did want to see him again, and weren't being polite without meaning.

'When can I come?' he said.

'When you see us,' said Leo. 'Don't forget our names.'

'Don't you, either,' said Rodney. Leo said he would try not to. Then he and the others ran away along the village street towards their houses.

Rodney went into Granny's house. Dinner was ready, and after dinner he had to write home, to tell Mother he had safely got to Grandfather's. He told her about Maureen Garley and the Three Bad Eggs, but it was hard to make tree climbing and sitting in a Nest sound exciting. He hoped Mother would understand without having to read a lot of words. He did not mention the noise and the trembling of the tree.

After his letter was finished he posted it. Then he helped Grandfather in the garden again. He spent a lot of time looking over into the common, and wondering whether he would hear the sound again, and feel the earth shake. Nothing happened. He thought that perhaps he was too far away from the dragon or the wolf.

Then he thought that dragons and wolves can walk. If they are strong enough to growl they are strong enough to get about. So the dragon, or the wolf, could very easily come out of the common, and into the village, into Grandfather's garden even, and then ...

He did not think what might happen next. Grandfather was asking him to come and help carry away a heap of pinched weeds from the flowerbeds, all wilting flowers and drooping leaves. Rodney arranged them on top of yesterday's grass, which was drying brown now, and getting warm.

He kept an eye on the common, waiting for movement in the trees. If a dragon came, perhaps it would do no harm. He wanted to see one. Perhaps it would only eat Maureen Garley, and nobody seemed to like Maureen Garley at all. It would not be fair if the dragon was unkind to her, too.

'Wake up,' said Grandfather. 'There's another basketful to take after that one.'

seven

The next morning Leo came to the door and asked whether Rodney could come out to play. Northman and Armadine stayed by the gate. Granny had a good look at Armadine to make sure she wasn't Maureen Garley, and said Rodney could go.

They went round on to the common along the road. Then they went carefully into the woods, looking out for two things: the noise, and Maureen Garley.

They did not hear the noise. But they saw Maureen. She was at the tree. She had pulled down the rope from the end of the branch, and she was just about to climb it.

The Three Bad Eggs and Rodney waited for a moment, while Leo thought out what to do. In the end there was no need to do anything, because Maureen Garley could not climb ropes. She tugged and she gripped and she swung, but she never got higher up than the first knot. Then she fell off. She got up and muttered to herself, and pulled and pulled at the rope until the branch swung high and low. She walked away when she had finished, and they saw her leave the common and go back into the village.

The Three Bad Eggs and Rodney climbed the tree, and stayed at the Nest all the morning. In the afternoon they went for an exploring walk in the woods, hoping to find interesting things. Leo led the way, and Rodney followed next. They saw squirrels and butterflies, and mice in the grass. They found four empty bottles and toadstools growing like a shelf all over a dead tree. Then they stopped and looked round the place they had got to.

'We've never been so far in before,' said Leo. 'Let's go a long way further in.'

Rodney thought the wood looked very happy and pretty, with the sun shining through the leaves overhead, and the birds singing round about, and all the stillness of summer lying under the trees. They all stood a little longer, because it was such a pleasant place to be in.

Northman began to open his mouth, as if he were going to speak.

But he did not speak. There was a shaking of the ground instead, and then the noise came, the roaring that they had heard the day before in the tree-top. Now it was much nearer, or perhaps they were nearer it. It was a long growl, going on and on, then fading away. The shaking of the ground went on longer.

And after the shaking had gone there came the cold breath of the thing that had made the noise, coming through the trees like a grey mist, and passing them by, and vanishing, leaving only its smell behind it, a smell that was old and thin and tired.

They all looked at each other, and walked gently away from that place, trying to follow their own track home.

When they had got a good way, Leo said: 'I didn't like that.'

'It must be moving about,' said Armadine, and that made them run a little way.

Rodney thought they were not going back the way they had come. On the way into the wood he had noticed white marks on some of the trees; and now the trees they were near had no white marks, and trees further away had them.

'All these trees have white marks,' said Leo. 'I don't know why. But I wasn't following them.'

Rodney looked again, and found that the trees nearby had marks, but they had been on the other side of the trunks. There were white splashes of paint, and numbers.

'Do you think IT did them?' said Armadine; and they had to hurry again. This time they didn't stop until they were out of the wood, and were among the low bushes and the grass and the village was in sight.

The next day Leo came alone for Rodney, and they played inside the village. Leo said it was just for a change, but Armadine said it was because of the dragon, or wolf. In the afternoon Rodney was invited to their real house in the village. He told Granny about it later.

'They don't live here,' he said. 'First I thought they lived in a tree, but they don't. They live in Coventry, and they come to stay with their auntie here. And there's

more than three of them. There's a baby one that's come
with them. It's not an absolute baby, because it runs about
and talks, and they call it Ann sometimes, and sometimes they call it Lickle, because it tries to say it's little,
but it doesn't know the word.'

'I thought I didn't know them,' said Granny. 'But I
thought I knew who they were, or I wouldn't have let
you go out with them.'

'They're all right,' said Rodney. 'They get frightened
of things, like dragons, that's all.' But he knew it was no
good talking of dragons to Granny. She would have
changed the subject at once.

The next day they were on the common again. They
had a war with Maureen Garley. She had failed to climb
the rope. But this time she brought a ladder with her,

and propped it against the branch, and went up that way. Rodney went to the tree first, and thought the Three Bad Eggs had brought the ladder, and he went up it. But before he got to the top of the tree Maureen had appeared from the roof of the Nest, and came to tread on his climbing hands, so that he had to go down again. But he took the ladder with him, and waited for the others to come.

'You don't need that,' said Leo, when he came, and saw the ladder. 'It's only Maureen Garley who would need that.'

'It was her,' said Rodney. 'And she's up there now.'

Maureen had driven Rodney from the tree. Before she had gone up she had cut the rope on the branch, and it was lying on the ground.

'It's her spiteful way,' said Armadine, picking up the rope. Now Maureen was up at the Nest, and making a lot of noise, banging and kicking. Rodney and Leo put the ladder up again, and climbed the tree. They took the rope with them, and caught Maureen. They tied the rope round her and made her climb down the tree, down the ladder, and let her go. She was very jealous, and said they hated her. Leo said they did. Maureen pulled the ladder down, took it by one rung, and walked off, dragging it after her.

'She's spoilt our last day,' said Leo. He had stayed in the tree to fasten the rope again. Then they all climbed up. 'We're going this afternoon,' he said. 'Now she's found the Nest I bet she spoils it for us before we come again.' They went to see whether she had spoilt it now; but she had only kicked it, and not even broken the window.

'We'll say goodbye to it,' said Armadine, 'and good luck.'

Northman smiled, and patted the hut on the roof. They waited for him to say something, but he didn't.

'Play our last play,' said Leo.

eight

Two mornings later Rodney woke early, and wondered where he was. He thought that if he was in Granny's house there was a lot of noise, and if he was at home there was not very much. His room was the same shape, and the bed in the same place in both houses. Then he remembered that he had come home, with his holiday over, and that tomorrow was the first day of school again. He looked forward to that, because everybody usually had to write a composition about the holiday they had just had, called 'What I did at half-term', or 'Christmas', or 'The Pantomime'. This time it would be the half-term one.

He wrote his composition, and it was the second best one in the class, and he had to read it out to the rest of them. No one believed in the dragon, though; but they didn't know what it could have been. He wrote to Grandfather, too, and asked about the aeroplane. Granny wrote back, when she was writing to Mother, and said that no one had come for the aeroplane yet, and it was getting dusty, because she did not like to touch it. She hoped someone would come soon, she told Mother.

So he went on going to school, day after day, waiting for the next holiday. Sometimes he would wake early in the morning, and sit up with his eyes closed, and open them, hoping that he would find himself at Grandfather's house. But he always found it was his own house he was in. Sometimes he walked to school in the rain, and thought how good it would be to sit in the Nest, high in the tree, while the rain poured down outside and rattled on the roof. Sometimes in the school playground he thought he heard Maureen Garley's voice, but when he looked it would be someone he knew already who had just sounded like that for a moment.

Then, one day in the summer holidays he was buying tickets at the station. This time there were two tickets to be got, a whole and a half, because Mother was coming. Rodney thought the man at the window with holes in it might remember him, but he did not seem to. Rodney paid him with a wrinkled and scented pound note from Mother's handbag.

Grandfather came down to Kenge station to meet them and carry Mother's case. Rodney's things were in the case too.

The first meal they had was tea, because they had come in the afternoon. After tea Rodney wanted to take Mother to see the Nest, and the tree it was in. Mother said she was too old to be climbing trees, and besides, she had been brought up at Kenge, in that very house, and she had been out on the common enough. She said she might have time to come out tomorrow, if Rodney was sure that his friends wouldn't mind if she saw the tree and the Nest.

'I don't think they would let you in,' said Rodney. 'I don't think you would get in. I just thought I would show you it before asking.'

'Who are his friends?' said Mother. 'Are there a whole lot of Garleys I don't know?'

'No,' said Rodney. 'Not her.'

'They've got another bad one, Maureen,' said Granny. 'But he's been going about with Millie Jenkins's lot. You remember Millie and her sister, don't you?'

Mother said she did, and there was a whole long talk then, over the last cup of tea, about people Mother had known when she was young. Grandfather got up and went into the garden. Rodney went after him.

'We can't live through all that chatter,' said Grandfather. 'It's like having sparrows tied to your ears.' He went to look at the runner beans. He thought he might have some with his supper.

Rodney went to the bottom of the garden, and looked over the fence. There was the common, and there was Maureen Garley walking through the grass, carrying something that looked like a small bucket. Rodney knew what it was. It was a paint pot, the sort that holds distemper. He could only think of one reason why Maureen should be going on to the common with a pot of wall paint. She must be going to paint a wall. And the only walls he knew in the common were the walls of the Nest.

He thought she must have got inside the Nest, and be making it into her own.

He got over the fence, and began to follow her.

She was going through the bushes now, and the trees were still ahead of her. Rodney bent low, ready to drop flat into the grass if she looked round.

She went straight on, swinging the paint pot in her right hand. Rodney saw that in her left hand she had a paint brush, with white paint on its bristles.

Maureen got into the wood. Rodney ran up to the bushes, and got among them. He would be out of sight now, and he could get closer to Maureen. At least, he found, he could have got closer if he had been able to walk

more quietly. But he seemed to be crashing through the wood rather like somebody being dragged along. He did not know that walking would make such a noise.

Maureen was in the clearing at the bottom of the oak tree. Rodney knew it was the same tree. He looked up into it, and saw the Nest.

Maureen was not trying to climb the tree. Rodney was going to wait until she was in the tree, and then he was going to order her out of it. If he waited until she was among the branches he would have more time to run away if she came for him.

She knelt on the ground, and began to stir the paint with a piece of wood. It was white paint. Rodney saw the piece of wood turn from brown to white. Then she dipped the brush into the pot, and made it painty. She stood up, walked to the trunk of the tree, and began to make a mark on it.

Then Rodney knew that she was making the same mark on the tree as the one they had seen in other places on the common. Maureen must have made them all, and he did not know why. Perhaps she was counting them.

Rodney would have painted the whole tree white, he thought. Maureen just made her mark. Rodney forgot she was the enemy, and stepped out into the clearing to ask her what she was doing. She did not smile, she did not answer. She stepped forward with her brush, dipped it in the paint, and made it ready. Then she painted a slappy white stripe right up Rodney's front, all the way up his body and straight up his face. Then, while he stood all surprised, she brushed his hair with it, and walked off.

nine

'I'm bigger than her,' said Mother. 'I'll give her such a bang when I catch her. It's the way you bring them up that makes the difference, and I don't suppose that Maureen Garley has been brought up at all, just left to run wild.' Mother was washing Rodney thoroughly in the bath when she spoke. The water was not very warm, and Mother was rubbing hard, mostly on Rodney's face. Granny was downstairs washing his trousers and his pullover, and they were both complaining because the paint did not want to come off in water.

'What possessed her to do such a thing I don't know,' said Mother, taking the bathroom jug and pouring chilly water over Rodney's hair. 'Well, we shan't get that bit out by washing. I shall have to cut it out with scissors. We can't have you going about with white hair like a little old man.'

Then she left him to finish himself, because only his head and his hands had had paint on them. She went downstairs to help Granny.

Rodney came down when he had finished, and had his supper in his pyjamas. His clothes were hanging outside on the clothes-line, to get the worst of the drips off them.

'We shall have to bring them in before night,' said Granny. 'It'll be raining before morning.'

The clothes were in before dark, but they still did not dry by morning. Rodney got up in the morning, but he could not get dressed, because he had only brought the clothes he wore on the way.

'You'll just have to stay in the house,' said Mother. 'You can't put wet clothes on. Even if you had them you'd still have to stay in, because of the rain.'

The rain was coming fast. It slapped against the windows, and it could be heard running in the road. It was not a cold day, and the kitchen window was open, because the rain was not coming from that side of the house. Rodney sat near it, and listened to the rain and wind on the common. He could not see the common because of the way the garden sloped up.

Then he wandered round the house, to see whether there was anything he could do. Granny did not have much for him to play with. Grandfather was the one with things to do, but today there was no gardening. Grandfather went for a wet walk by himself. He had to leave Rodney behind. Rodney helped Mother and Granny have their elevenses. He felt his clothes, which were hanging by a small fire. They were not drying very quickly, he thought, because the fire was too small. But it was a warm day, and Granny said she was sorry, but she could not bear to have a big fire on a day like that.

Rodney walked round the bedrooms, to see whether he could find anything interesting there. His own room had nothing in it but three dolls and a doll's house, which used to belong to Mother when she was small. He did not want to play with them himself. The only house he wanted to play with was the Nest, and he did not really want to play there by himself. Two of the dolls spoke when he picked them up and leaned them over. The third one did not wake up at all, though its eyes were wide open all the time. He put them all back, and went into the next room.

There he remembered what he had forgotten for a long time. The aeroplane. He stood on Granny's bed, with his feet sinking into the eiderdown, and looked on to the top of the wardrobe. The black and yellow striped aeroplane was there, sitting by the boots, getting dusty. It had never moved since it was put there. So no one had come for it.

He ran downstairs and asked Granny about it. She was peeling potatoes. She said she had never heard a thing from anybody about it, and she said that perhaps it was time to go to the police station and ask; and the best time to do that was after tea.

'Can I get it down now, and not play with it?' said Rodney. 'Just dust it and look at it, and show Mother.'

'I'll lift it down,' said Granny. 'Come on.' She dried her hands, and they went upstairs for it. She lifted it

down, and told him to carry it carefully, and they would blow the dust off it outside. He took it sideways downstairs, and out to the kitchen door, and they both blew clouds of dust away from it. Then he carried it carefully back into the room, where Mother was ironing his trousers for him. He put it on the table, and let Mother look at it. He dusted it with a soft cloth Granny gave him, and showed Mother how it worked. Then he and Granny put it on the sideboard, between the salt and pepper stand and the shiny biscuit barrel, and it stood on its own reflection.

After dinner he got dressed, and began to wait for tea, not because he was hungry, but because after tea they would be going to the police station.

The rain stopped. Mother said she was going out for a breath of fresh air, and to see how the old place was getting on. 'And if I see that Maureen Garley, well,' she said, 'I shall know her. You can't mistake a Garley.'

Rodney went with her. They walked up the road, because Mother wanted to have a look at the common first, though she thought she would not go on to it in the wet. Grandfather said it was very muddy at the moment, when there was the slightest bit of rain.

Mother and Rodney went to the road to the common, and walked up it. But they didn't get to the common. For one thing it started to rain again, a little bit, and for another, it was a narrow road, and it was full of a big wagon, dragging a load of cut trees behind it. It was the sort of wagon that is a front end by itself, and then there is a hinge, or swinging part, and then, a long way back, more wheels.

'Articulated,' said Mother.

The wagon was made of trees, really, because there was no body at the back. There was a load of trees, and the back wheels were at the far end of the trunks, and there was nothing else to hold the wheels on but the trees themselves. The wagon was coming out of the common, slowly, sinking into the road a little way and throwing up mud. It made the mud as it came, by squashing the water of the rain into the ground. Mother and Rodney came out of the road to the common, and stood aside, to let the timber go by. Then Mother said the road was too bad to walk on, and she would look at the common another time, and they went down into the village.

ten

Down by the post office they met Maureen Garley. She was sitting on a wall in the rain. Mother said it must be a Garley as soon as she saw her. Rodney said it was the very one, and the only one he had met.

'There were some very tough ones when I was young,' said Mother. 'This one will be their descendant.' And then, instead of doing all the things she had threatened, such as a good smack, or a talking to, or shaking some sense into her, Mother smiled at Maureen, and walked by.

'It's no good,' she said. 'Everybody hates Garleys, and I'm sure it isn't fair. I know she painted you, and I know she isn't pleasant to your friends; but I'm sorry for her, because she's a Garley, and that's not much fun.'

'She's bigger than me,' said Rodney. 'So I don't think about her at all. She can do what she likes.'

'She'll catch cold, sitting there,' said Mother.

Then they went into the post office and bought a bar of chocolate from the old people who kept it, and Mother talked to them about the time long before Rodney was alive when she had been a girl. The old people looked at Rodney, and said he was getting a big boy. Rodney waited patiently. He had his eye on the chocolate. When they got outside they broke into it and ate it as they went along.

The chocolate did not spoil their tea. They had that as soon as they got back. After that Rodney was waiting and waiting for Granny to put her coat on and go with him to the police station about the aeroplane. Instead of doing anything like that, Granny set to and washed up.

Rodney sat with Grandfather. They were talking about the mud in the road to the common, and the timber wagon that had filled the road.

'They're doing some clearing,' said Grandfather. 'You see, the common belongs to the village, and the village wants some money for different things.'

'I didn't know villages wanted money,' said Rodney. 'I thought people wanted money.'

'The village is made of people,' said Grandfather. 'The people want the money to rebuild a wall by the road, and they want money to pay for the street lamps, and to put gates at the edge of the common, to stop cows wandering out into the road. Cows, or horses, or other animals that go on the common to eat grass. So the village has sold some of the trees on the common to make money, and the timber wagons are taking the trees away.'

'Oh,' said Rodney. 'Will they take all the trees?'

'If you look over the fence,' said Grandfather, 'you won't be able to see any difference at all. All the trees they are taking are further away.'

That was a good thing, Rodney thought. It meant that the tree with the Nest in would be safe. He knew that he could see the garden from the tree, so he was sure he would be able to see the tree from the garden. 'I didn't want them to take down just one particular tree,' he said.

'That big old oak where you play,' said Grandfather. 'No, that will be safe enough, but there are some the other side of it that will go.'

'I shall go and watch tomorrow,' said Rodney. 'Can I?'

'If you don't get underneath a falling tree,' said Grandfather. 'But you'd better ask your mother as well.'

Rodney went to ask Mother; but when he came to the kitchen and the sink, Granny was just washing her hands before putting on her coat.

'Yes, yes,' she said. 'We're ready to go now. Are you going to bring the thing with you?'

'It might get wet,' said Rodney. It was still raining a little outside. He thought that water might shrink some part of the aeroplane, like the plastic. And he thought too that if they took the aeroplane they might have to leave it at the police station while somebody thought about it. It would be safer on the sideboard where it was. Grandfather would never touch it.

They went out and walked along the wet road. Rodney noticed that their reflections were like the reflection of the aeroplane on the sideboard. They were standing on their own colours in the shininess of the road.

There was a different policeman at the police station. The last one had been big and dark. Today's one was small and dark. He said there had been a change since the summer, and he was here now. Granny called him 'Young man', but in her kind voice, the one she used for people like cats.

The young man said he would look in the book, and when was it that they had come before, and what had they brought?

Granny explained, until they came to the part about aeroplanes, and then Rodney thought he had better join in and explain better. No one could expect Granny to know about aeroplanes.

The policeman looked in his books, and found a place where something was written down. Then he had a look at the calendar.

'I'm sorry,' he said, looking again at the book to make sure. 'I'm very sorry.'

'Oh,' said Rodney. 'And I did want it.'

'I'm sorry I didn't come round and tell you about it,' said the policeman. 'I should have been round a fortnight ago to tell you that no one has claimed the aeroplane, you can keep it.'

'There you are, Rodney,' said Granny, 'you made your mind up too soon. It's yours.'

'Mine,' said Rodney. And he was so glad that his face went red, and his legs went red, and his mouth began to move about by itself, and his nose tickled, and a tear got out of his eye and ran down his cheek beside his nose and into his mouth, and tasted of salt.

'There now,' said the policeman, patting him on the back. 'I said it all the wrong way about, didn't I? What if you have a blow of my whistle, and then you'll feel better; and you can go back to your aeroplane.'

So Rodney had a blow of the whistle, and Granny covered her ears, and Rodney felt better, and they went home. The rain washed away the feeling of the tear on his cheek, and his blush went back inside him. And he had a black and yellow striped aeroplane that belonged to him.

eleven

In the morning, when breakfast was over, and Mother was awake enough to be asked about it, Rodney went on to the common with the aeroplane.

'Do you know how to work it?' said Grandfather.

'I worked it last night,' said Rodney. 'Didn't I?'

Grandfather agreed that Rodney had worked the aeroplane last night. What he had done was wind up the elastic of the propeller, and let the propeller turn round, and blown all Grandfather's pipe smoke away from him with the fan draught of it. The draught had blown away all the flimsy paper that Mother and Granny had laid out on the table ready for cutting out a dress. It had all had to be picked up again.

'I just thought it might need adjusting, somehow,' said Grandfather. 'But I don't know how to do it.'

'Nor do I,' said Rodney. He wished he did. 'But I'll just try it.'

He went round by the road, and on to the grassy part of the common. Part of the grass was torn up by the wheels of the wood wagons. He went away from that part, because his shoes were sticking in the mud. He went behind the houses, and looked along the fence at the back of the gardens. There was a lot of grass here, between the beginning of the trees and the garden fence.

He wound the propeller of the aeroplane, but not as tight as he could have wound it, in case he broke it. Then he lifted the aeroplane high overhead with one hand, held the propeller with the other, and launched the machine.

It flew. It swooped. It turned a corner. It just missed the fence, and it landed upside down in the grass. Rodney thought it would have landed the right way up if the grass had been as short as the grass in Grandfather's garden, where he had seen it land before. He picked it up. There was no spin left in the propeller.

He wound it again, a little tighter this time, and tried

once more. This time the aeroplane flew straight, and went upwards a little. Then it stopped in mid-air, and fell down to the ground, spinning. It had stopped because the propeller had stopped first. He ran after it, and tried again, winding as tight as he could this time.

There were controls on the aeroplane. There was a rudder that could be moved. There were long hinged pieces on the wings. He tried an experiment, with one wing having its hinge up and one wing having it down, and the rudder turned to one side. The aeroplane flew round in a circle, going up first, then down and landing suddenly in the grass, the right way up. He tried the same setting again, and this time the aeroplane turned upside-down very soon and fell out of the air. When he picked it up, the propeller whizzed

round and knocked the back of his fingers.

He had a rest. He had run about too much. He walked along the fence, and looked over to see whether Grandfather was watching at all. But there was no one in the garden. He walked back to the road on to the common, and watched a timber trailer coming in with its engine roaring. He heard the biting of axes down in the woodland, and watched a man mending a petrol-driven saw, and went away when he heard it start up, because the noise was very loud. He heard other saws like it among the trees. They sounded more like wolves, he thought, when they tore into the trees. He remembered the other noise that he and the Three Bad Eggs had heard before, and for a moment he thought that the unknown noise was not so bad or so frightening. Then he remembered how the earth shook with it, and he had to look towards the trees and listen with his feet. But there was nothing.

He wound the propeller again, and then had to hold the aeroplane awkwardly while he set the controls quite straight, as if they were not there at all. Then he launched it again, and watched it go.

It flew straight and steady, going higher and higher, along the grassy place between the trees and the fence. He ran along after it. Then he stopped, and just watched it, because if he was running he could not see it.

It climbed up, and then it began to sink down, gently coming closer to the ground. The propeller stopped turning. The aeroplane came down and down, and landed as if it had a pilot, and sat against the edge of the forest like a real thing.

Rodney stood and looked at it. It was his first really good and successful flight, with a good launching, a good going, and a good coming down. That was what aeroplanes were for. He went towards it a little way, and stopped to look again. It was there, and he had put it there. He had flown it there. This minute, he thought, was what he had waited for ever since the aeroplane landed for the first time.

Then Maureen Garley stepped out from the bushes at the edge of the trees, walked over to the aeroplane, and picked it up.

Rodney shouted, and began to run. But suddenly he found he did not dare go much nearer Maureen Garley. She might twist him, or paint him, or even hit him with the aeroplane. That would be the worst thing because it would damage the aeroplane too, and damage it more than him.

Maureen Garley did not run away. She was doing something to the aeroplane. He did not know what she was doing. She would be doing something very bad to it, he knew. She looked as if she was breaking something off it. Then she held it up, and he was sure she was holding it much too tight. She touched the wings, and she touched the tail. And she launched the aeroplane into the air, and it flew back towards Rodney. It went overhead, climbing as it passed, and then it began to descend. It made another perfect landing. This time Rodney ran to it and got there first, and looked to see what harm had been done.

No harm had been done at all. The aeroplane was perfect, Maureen Garley had not hurt it at all. He picked it up, and turned round to see what she was doing. She was standing in the same place. She was looking at him.

'Hey,' she shouted, 'send it again. It's good, isn't it?'

Rodney wound the propeller up, set the controls straight and sent the aeroplane off again. It was better with two, he thought, and even if one was Maureen Garley she seemed to have done everything right. She clapped her hands, and the aeroplane climbed into the sky again.

twelve

The aeroplane was high up, being driven gently along by its propeller. Rodney's eyes were flying with it, and looking down on a tiny world. His real self stood on the ground and swayed from side to side, and his hands turned the little figure-of-eight wheel that aeroplanes have. There was an engine noise going on. Rodney was making it with his throat. The landing-field that he was making for was Maureen Garley.

Then his attention was taken quite away from the aeroplane. He did not even have time to tell it to go on by itself. It just went on. There was a noise that he was not making himself, a large noise.

He thought for a moment it was going to be the noise of the thing in the wood, the dragon or wolf. But it was not that. It was the noise of one of the petrol-driven saws, starting up close by. By the time Rodney had realized what it was, roaring, the aeroplane had landed, and was out of sight.

He glanced to where it would be, and waited for Maureen to send it back. While he did that he looked to see where the saw was being used. He thought, though, that it was not yet being used to cut wood, only for a test. He heard the clip-clop of an axe on wood, and heard the flakes of wood fly out, and a woodman whistling to himself.

He thought there might be a tree falling in a moment, and he wanted to go and see about it. But first he had to wait for the aeroplane to come back. It did not come. He stood and looked for it, expecting to see it fly up from Maureen's hand and swim its way towards him.

Then he saw that Maureen was not there. She was not winding the propeller up, she was not preparing to launch, she was not there to wave to him and shout out that it was fun. She had gone. And no one had sent the aeroplane back.

'She's taken it with her,' Rodney shouted; though there

was no one to hear him. The axe went on chopping among the trees, and the woodman went on whistling. Rodney ran to where the aeroplane should be, knowing in his heart that it would not be there at all, that Maureen would have stolen it and taken it away, and that he should never have let her touch it at all.

The aeroplane was sitting in the grass, with its elastic slack. No one had stolen it, no one had taken it away. Maureen had gone by herself.

'Well, I don't care,' said Rodney to himself, but not so loudly, not shouting this time. 'She shouldn't have gone away like that.' He was still angry with her. He picked the aeroplane up and looked at it carefully. It was in good health. He took it to the fence behind the houses, and put it over on to the compost heap, on top of some smelly purple onion flowers. He looked round to see what he should do about Maureen.

He was not cross any more. The aeroplane was safe, and he had played with it long enough today. He stopped leaning on the fence, and went back on to the common.

The axe was still being used. He followed the noise. He went to it by a way he knew, along the track that would bring him to the oak tree where the Nest was. It was not really a marked track, but the way he knew. He worked out that the noise was coming from further away than the oak tree.

He was wrong. The noise was happening at the oak tree itself. The axe that was biting wood out was biting it from the trunk of the tree that had the Nest in it. Under the tree stood a man with a petrol saw, waiting to have his turn at the tree.

'Hey,' said Rodney, in the biggest voice he had. Not the loudest voice, but the most mannish and ordering-aboutish voice.

'Hey to you,' said the man with the saw.

'That's our tree,' said Rodney. 'It's where we have our Nest. You can't cut that down.'

The man with the saw walked up to the tree. He pointed with the spiky end of the saw blade to the trunk. 'That's our mark,' he said. 'We cut to that. That's our orders and our contract.'

'That's what we have to do,' said the man with the axe, pausing between two blows. Then the axe bit again.

'What's your mark?' said Rodney, because the saw had been pointing to the mark that Maureen Garley had made with white paint. 'That isn't a proper mark. You didn't put it there.'

'I know I didn't,' said the man with the saw. 'And I wouldn't if I could. But the mark's there, and we have to take this tree.'

Rodney said that the mark was not a proper one, and that Maureen Garley had made it. The man said that the mark was the mark they were working to, and he could go and show Rodney dozens more like it in the common, and those were the trees that had to be taken. The man with the axe went on slicing wood white from the tree. Rodney showed the saw-man the Nest, high among the branches. The saw-man said that tree houses were nothing to do with him, and that Rodney shouldn't have built it in a tree with a white mark on.

Then Rodney was very angry again, because he knew that the tree should not be chopped down, and he knew that Maureen had only put the mark there for spite. He wanted to be angry with Maureen, only she was not there. He had to be angry with the woodmen. He was so cross that the man with the axe stopped chopping. When he did, Rodney went and stood against the gash in the tree, where the axe had eaten its way in. 'Now,' he said, 'you can't chop.'

'If you were my boy,' said the man with the axe, 'I'd go and chop myself a big stick, and take it to you, and you'd see what I meant.'

The saw-man had been thinking, when Rodney was so angry. 'I wonder,' he said. 'You know, when they chose the trees, they won't have seen that hut. You wait here, you two, and I'll be back directly.' He put down his saw, and went off among the trees.

He came back riding on the front part of one of the articulated wood wagons, banging through the trees and over the rough ground, and coming right up to the foot of the oak. He got out, nodded to Rodney, picked up his saw, and climbed up the wagon and into the tree. He took with him, as well, the end of a rope, which was round a winch at the back of the cab. He shouted to Rodney to stand away from under. Then there was a lot of sawing noise high in the tree, and a rain of white sawdust, and a big rustling. Then there was a lot of shouting, and running of the wagon engine, and down on the rope came the Nest, still fastened to its branches, with the branches no longer fastened to the tree. The Nest settled on the ground, and tilted over. Things inside it rolled about. Then the saw-man and his saw came down the tree, and asked Rodney where he would like the Nest put now.

thirteen

Rodney came back to the house late for his dinner. Granny looked at him without a smile.

'He's been good up to now,' she said to Mother. 'I hope he doesn't spoil it all now.'

'Where's your aeroplane, Rodney?' said Mother, because she thought he should have it with him.

Rodney said it was in the garden, and that he hadn't forgotten it. Granny said he had better go and get his hands washed, because he wasn't having his dinner when he was that colour, no matter what time of day it was. Grandfather lit his pipe and said nothing. He rattled the newspaper and that was all.

Rodney was not allowed to talk while he ate. Granny watched him all the time, waiting for him to finish the plateful, so that she could wash the plate. Rodney wanted to talk, but he had to wait until his last mouthful of pudding was in and swallowed. Before the lump of it had settled in his chest he was able to begin.

'We put it in another tree,' he said. 'I helped. I told them how to do it.'

Granny thought he was talking about the aeroplane. Mother knew him better, she said, and waited to see what he said before thinking what it was about.

'We have to have the whole story first,' she said.

'Rodney, you're like your mother was,' said Granny. 'Tell it your way out.'

Rodney began to explain, how he had flown the aeroplane, how Maureen Garley had helped him, and sent it back, and then gone away.

'You can never tell with a Garley,' said Mother. 'Here today, gone tomorrow, and not back again yesterday.'

Rodney told them about the mark on the tree, and got them very confused when he tried to tell them that Maureen had put the mark there. They said she couldn't have done, because it wasn't her business. Mother reminded Granny that nothing was a Garley's business, most of the time, but that didn't stop them from being in it.

Rodney skipped over the part where he had stood with his back to the gash on the tree and shouted at the woodmen. He had forgotten what he said at the time, in any case. He thought it was something like 'Big stupid people cutting down every big stupid thing you big stupidly see in the big stupid wood.' He was ashamed now at himself for behaving like that, and he hoped no one would ever know about it. Perhaps he had only thought he was shouting, and had only been whispering or thinking, and the woodmen had heard nothing, and would tell nobody. All he told Granny and Mother was that he had asked the men to move the Nest from the tree.

'Did they?' said Mother. 'It was very good of them if they did.'

'They sawed it down, with all its branches round it,' said Rodney. 'And then they sawed the branches off it, and then they pulled it away to another tree, and they lifted it up with the rope, and put it in the branches again.'

'Did you say thank you?' said Grandfather. Rodney thought for a moment.

'I think so,' he said. 'They said I could come and watch them again, so I must have, mustn't I?'

'Go on,' said Mother. 'What happened next?'

'I was late for my dinner,' said Rodney. 'I couldn't help it, could I?'

Grandfather had a few words to say about not standing in the wrong place when trees were being cut down. He gave Rodney an explanation about falling trees, but Rodney did not understand it very well. He said he would be careful, though, and went off again, to see how the woodmen were doing.

The saw was singing and biting at wood when he went on to the common. He could smell the sap of a tree, heavy in the air, sometimes sharp and fresh, sometimes cooked and heavy, where the whizzing blade had warmed it.

The tree he could smell was the oak tree. He came to the edge of the clearing, and wondered where he should stand, because Grandfather's explanation hadn't been any help. The explanation had been more about how Grandfather's smoking-pipe would fall if tiny woodmen sawed it down, than about how a real tree would fall. But the woodmen saw him, and told him where to stand. He watched the tree having its trunk severed and wedged, and then the rope put among its branches again. The rope was still on the winch on the wagon. The men thought they had sawed enough, in the end, and came to the wagon, started the engine and turned the handle on the winch. The rope began to pull. It pulled straight. Little branches and twigs broke off in the top of the tree, where the rope pulled itself tight like a rod. Then the tree cried out, and Rodney looked all round him to see whether there was anyone else who would tell him what to think. The tree had suddenly become like a person to him, speaking unexpectedly and asking for help.

There was Maureen Garley, standing a little way behind him, and looking up at the tree too. She had a hand to her mouth and her eyes wide open. She looked at the tree, she looked at Rodney.

'It's hurting it,' she said. 'It's hurting it ever so much,' and her eyes had tears in them, and the tears ran on to her face.

The tree cried out again, and then gave a yawning noise, and fell over like a giant sneeze, shaking the earth.

Wood and dry oak leaves whirled in the air, and the branches all fell in on themselves.

'Oh,' said Maureen. 'I liked that part.' She shook her head, and the tears vanished. The winch stopped turning, and there was a moment of silence in the wood.

Then there was the noise that Rodney had heard before, the wolf or dragon noise, and the shaking of the ground. He and Maureen looked at each other, and then at the woodmen.

'It's something or other,' said the axe-man. 'I don't know what. I don't worry, I don't have to be here at night.'

Maureen nodded with her head, to mean that she wanted Rodney to come away. Rodney tiptoed away after her, listening for the noise again. It spoiled the day, he thought, to have it coming again when he had forgotten about it. 'I'm frightened,' he said, and he ran out of the wood and into the grassy place of the common, where Maureen waited for him.

fourteen

'Well,' said Maureen. 'That wasn't bad.'

'You did it,' said Rodney. 'You marked the tree with the mark, and they had to cut it down.'

'I know,' said Maureen. 'But you don't like those kids either, do you. That house will all be broken up now.'

'Oh,' said Rodney. 'Will it?'

'Yes,' said Maureen. 'And they can't really blame me, can they, because I didn't touch it, did I? It just came down with the tree.'

'You ought to be sorry,' said Rodney. 'It wasn't your tree.'

'And it isn't yours either,' said Maureen. 'So let's go and play with that aeroplane, because that isn't yours either. They can take it away from you, you know, it isn't yours. My dad said so, and he knows, because the real owner can have it if he wants to, so they can take it away, and they will, I know they will, so let's go and play with it. I know who it really belongs to, and I'll tell them where it is if you don't play with it now, and then you'll lose it.'

Rodney had heard people at school talk like that before now, and he was sure it didn't mean anything. It was only a way of making people do things. But he wanted to play with the aeroplane now, and he did what Maureen said, fetching it from the other side of the fence, winding up the propeller, and launching it off towards the trees.

He was standing in the grass watching its return flight, and imagining that he was in it, when something took hold of his ankle, tightly.

The whole world jumped with him, and his skin went tight all down his back, and he tried to jump into the air.

'Look out,' said a voice. 'You'll tread on my hand.'

Rodney looked down. Lying in the grass behind him was Leo, with one hand on Rodney's ankle. 'We stalked you,' he said. 'Is that your dad's aeroplane? Is he sending it back?'

The aeroplane landed twenty feet away. Leo let go of the ankle, and Rodney went for the aeroplane.

'Let's see it,' said Leo, sitting up on the grass and putting up his hand. 'Can I send it to him?' He got up, and looked towards the trees. 'That isn't your dad,' he said. 'That's Maureen Garley. You're playing with Maureen Garley. Susan,' he shouted. 'I mean Armadine, it's Maureen Garley, come away. Northman, come back.'

He handed the aeroplane back to Rodney. Away in the grass two people stood up, Armadine and Northman. They were halfway towards Maureen, stalking her in the way Leo had stalked Rodney. Maureen saw them too, and began to pick up stones and throw them. But they were very small stones, and the distance was too big.

'We are going to our private tree house,' said Leo. 'You needn't come. We don't want you.'

'But I'm not friends with her,' said Rodney. 'She made me play with her.'

Leo laughed a false and scornful laugh. Armadine came up to them then. 'It's her,' she said. 'Maureen.' Northman followed, and pointed his thumb towards Maureen, which meant that he agreed.

'He's gone over to her side,' said Leo. pointing at Rodney. 'He says she made him.'

'That's the sort of thing she does,' said Armadine. 'But he might just be saying that.'

Rodney had been ready to tell them what Maureen had done with their tree; but when Armadine thought he might be like Maureen he decided at once to say nothing more, because it would be difficult, and difficulties had gone on long enough today. 'It's tea-time,' he said, without looking at any of the Three Bad Eggs. He picked up the aeroplane, and walked off towards the fence, put the aeroplane over, and climbed after it. He looked back when he was over. The Three Bad Eggs were walking towards the wood, and the place where their tree should be, and the Nest in the tree.

It was nowhere near tea-time. He spent the rest of the afternoon in the garden, not flying the aeroplane, but having it on the aerodrome of the lawn, a jungle clearing, with the stray but famous Grandfather giant walking about among the trees frightening all the inhabitants.

Once or twice he looked over the fence. The second time he saw the Three Bad Eggs walking out of the common, looking very quiet and glum. They all seemed as silent as Northman. Then, later on, he heard a noise at the fence, and saw something bobbing beyond it. He went to it and looked over, hoping it would be Leo. It was Maureen.

'Come on,' she said. 'Quick.'

'No,' said Rodney. 'Not with you.'

'No, it's true,' said Maureen. 'Come with me. I daren't go alone, and I've got to. It's one of those kids, the little

one, and it's got lost in the wood, and there's that noise, and I can't go in alone.'

'It's a trick,' said Rodney. 'But I'll come. If it isn't a trick, I'll believe you, but if it is I won't.'

It was not a trick. Maureen ran across the grass, and in among the trees. Then she ran more slowly, and so did Rodney, in case they disturbed the thing that made the noise.

'It was this way,' Maureen whispered. 'She followed the other ones, and they didn't know, and she'll get lost, I know she will, and they're sure to blame me.' Rodney thought they might blame him, too.

Then they heard someone crying softly, down in the shadows among the big trees. It was someone in a white dress, sitting at the foot of the biggest tree of all. It was Leo's little sister, the one called Ann or Lickle. She was lost.

She was easy to rescue. She put a hand up for each of them to hold, and said she wanted to go home. Maureen bent over, though, picked her up. 'I'll carry you,' she said. 'Now we'll take you home.'

Rodney touched the big tree. It was not a big tree at all. It had no branches. It went up three times as tall as Rodney, and it was made of stone. It was a round stone tower, in among the trees, and the place in the woods where it was, seemed to be the darkest place there was.

They were out of the wood very soon. There was no noise of wolf or dragon. When they were all three in the grass again it was daylight once more, and they saw the Three Bad Eggs running across the common towards them.

Leo was there first. 'Give her back at once,' he said. 'You shouldn't have taken her.'

'Don't be daft,' said Maureen. 'We didn't. We just went in and got her.'

'She was lost,' said Rodney.

'I know,' said Armadine, putting out her hands to Ann. 'Come on, pet.' But Ann did not come. She wanted to hold on to Maureen.

'I'll carry her,' said Maureen. 'Won't I?' And the little girl's arms went round Maureen's neck again.

'Hey, where's our tree?' said Northman, suddenly 'Eh?'

'And our house?' said Leo. 'Do you know?'

'Yes,' said Rodney. 'They chopped your tree down. But Maureen and I made them take the Nest out first and put it somewhere else, didn't we, Maureen?'

'Yes,' said Maureen. 'We've done all sorts of things you don't know about. Shall I carry your baby home?'

'Yes,' said Leo. 'But, well, don't say we lost her, will you? We aren't supposed to lose her.'

'If you'll be friends,' said Maureen. 'And if you don't mind my bad temper I won't mind yours.'

'That'll be all right,' said Leo. 'What did you do with our Nest?'

'Oh, he knows,' said Maureen.

'I know,' said Rodney. 'But I know about another thing too, something I just found in the wood, and I think it's better than a Nest, but more frightening.'

'There's five of us now,' said Leo. 'Not counting Lickle. That's more than can be frightened, isn't it?'

fifteen

Rodney borrowed long nails from Grandfather in the morning, and the hammer called the garden hammer, which Grandfather used outdoors, leaving the smart one indoors. The nails were to fasten the Nest to its new tree. It had been nailed to the branches of the old tree, and it still was, where the branches had not been cut away.

The other Bad Eggs were going to bring a saw and an axe, and some clothes-line, to tie the Nest firmly in its new place.

Rodney met them at the entrance of the common, and they were there just at the time when their old tree was being taken away, massive on its wagon.

'We should take our hats off, I think,' said Leo. 'People do, don't they?'

But they were not wearing hats, so they could not do anything. Maureen Garley was there. She was bringing something Rodney did not quite understand about, to make the floor level. But she looked as if she had brought nothing at all, unless she had it in the pocket of the jacket she was wearing.

Leo waved the axe. 'They wouldn't let me bring it until I promised not to use it,' he said. 'But I thought I'd better bring it.' Armadine had a saw, and Northman had coiled the clothes-line round one shoulder and across his chest. Rodney carried the long nails between his fingers like steel claws until they began to hurt him. He put them back in his pocket.

The new tree where the Nest was was another oak, not so big as the first one, but easier to climb. The Nest itself lay crooked in a fork, with its door out towards the open air, and not reachable. They had a great deal of difficult work to do before they could even get in.

They did it gradually, with the help of broken branches from other trees, which they sawed to better lengths, and used as levers. Leo forgot after a time that he had not to use the axe. He was soon chopping away with it,

trimming awkward twigs from the oak tree, and awkward corners from the hut itself. They gradually brought the door round to a better side, to where you did not need to be a flyer to get to it. Then Leo unlocked it, and they began to go in.

They had to leave before they had done much levelling. The thing Maureen had brought would not do the work for them, which was a pity. All it would do was tell them when the floor was level. It never did say that, either. All it would say was that the floor was not level. The thing was a spirit level, which is a piece of wood with a glass tube in the side, with green liquid in the tube, and a bubble in the liquid. When the bubble is in the middle of the tube, then the wood is lying level. If it goes to one end, or out of sight, then the thing is not level.

'After dinner,' said Leo, 'we'll do something else.'

'Like flying the aeroplane,' said Rodney.

'That's what I meant,' said Leo. 'And what is the other thing you said you had found, Rodney?'

'I'll show that to you as well,' said Rodney.

And then the tree shook and the noise came out of the wood, and after the noise there was the dry smell that they had smelt before.

'There's five of us,' said Leo. 'We are not afraid.'

'Of course not,' said Maureen. 'Let's go home. You know we have to because it's time, and you're all frightened but I'm not.' But it was Maureen who fell out of the tree before she reached the lowest branch and dropped the spirit level, so that it broke. She was down first, and they found her looking at the ground and feeling for something.

'Mind the broken glass,' she said. 'I'm looking for the bubble. That's the part I'm not meant to lose. My dad told me not to lose the bubble.'

'I think it was a joke,' said Leo, when he had thought.

'Oh,' said Maureen, and grew cross with them all.

In the afternoon Rodney brought the aeroplane, and they flew it across the grass. Then Leo thought they should be more adventurous with it, and they flew it in a glade of the wood, and then they flew it in a little clearing that held a tiny pond. Leo was clever with the aeroplane. He could set its controls very accurately, and make it fly round in small circles, so that it went overhead three times before landing again.

Then Leo grew tired of winding the propeller. 'Show us the thing you found,' he said, handing the aeroplane to Rodney. 'What is it?'

'You'll see,' said Maureen, though she did not know either. But she was bigger than Leo, and sometimes had to show it, even if she had to let him be the leader of everybody.

'It's where we found Lickle,' said Rodney. Maureen knew where she had begun, and they followed her into the wood. The wood grew thicker, and the path went uphill. Rodney remembered that they had come more quickly last time, and he did not notice the hill. It had been darker, too, and he had not seen everything.

Now it was just a hilly woodland walk. He did not know whether he had been that way before. Then he knew he hadn't because they came out into an open place. Leo wanted to know if this was the thing. Rodney looked round and said it wasn't. Leo took the aeroplane, wound it up, and let it have a fly. Rodney looked round the edges of the open space. And there he saw the tower again, by accident, because his eye had been following the aeroplane as much as anything. Or perhaps the aeroplane had been following his eye, because it went straight towards the tower, over the top of it, and out of sight.

'That's it,' said Rodney. 'It looks like a tree, but it isn't. It's a tower.'

The others had to touch the tower to make sure it was not wooden. It was solid stone. They walked all round it, and tried to find a door. There was no door. The tower stood at the edge of the clearing alone, with no doors and no windows. Leo tried to climb it, but it was too smooth. All he could do with it was look at it. When they had looked at it they looked for the aeroplane.

The aeroplane had gone. They looked for a long time but they could not find it. It had lost itself again.

sixteen

'Did they hit you?' said Maureen the next day, when she met Rodney.

'No,' said Rodney. He knew what Maureen meant. 'I didn't tell anyone.'

'They hit me for losing that bubble,' said Maureen. 'It wasn't all that much of a joke.'

Armadine had something on her mind all the morning. She was trying to tell Leo to do something. Northman was stopping work now and then and looking at Leo, talking to him only with his eyes. Leo always looked away from both of them. The work was the same as yesterday's, but a little easier in some ways, because they did not have to worry about being exactly level. They jerked the Nest about until the branches of the tree rustled, and wedged the little hut firmly in the fork. Then Rodney brought out the nails, which were still in his pocket, along with the hammer, and they nailed the hut to the tree wherever it touched, until it would not slide about any more.

Then the work stopped. There was an odd silence. Leo had something on his mind, anyone could tell that. The others in his family knew what it was, but they were not going to say. Rodney could not guess what they were thinking. He hoped it was not anything unfriendly, that was all.

Leo put his hand in his pocket. Then he took it out again.

'This afternoon,' he said, and his voice wasn't quite his own, 'we'll have another good look for your aeroplane, Rodney.'

'Yes,' said Rodney. 'If you like.'

Armadine looked at Leo as if Leo had told the biggest lie in the world. Northman stared at him, and opened his mouth, but did not make a sound when it was open. He closed it again and grunted.

'Dinner-time,' said Leo, and he began to whistle as he climbed down the tree. Armadine and Northman followed him down, then Maureen. She looked at Rodney and shook her head, and she meant: there's something funny going on.

At the edge of the common they did not part and run off cheerfully in different directions, as they had yesterday. All they did was look at each other and then look away, and say, 'After dinner then', and walk off without any more words of farewell.

Leo walked away alone, with Armadine and Northman together behind him.

Rodney had a feeling he would never see them again. But after dinner they were there, at the entrance to the common, and the Three Bad Eggs were quarrelling. He heard them talking angrily to each other. The other two were attacking Leo, with words, not with their fists. He was being stubborn. He walked away from them and came to Rodney.

'We'll have a good look,' he said. 'That'll be best.'

They did have a good look. They went down yesterday's path to the clearing. They could see where they had walked in the clearing, because the tall grass was dying now and did not recover when it had been trodden down. They saw the paths they had made, and the circle they had trampled round the tower. They remembered where they had stood, as nearly as they could, when the aeroplane had vanished. They looked carefully along the line where the aeroplane should have gone. But there was no trace of it.

'That's it,' said Armadine, when they had come into the clearing, and gone out again beyond the tower, and were among the trees deep in the wood. 'That's it,' she said. 'Tell him, Leo.'

Northman nodded in agreement.

Leo put his hand in his pocket. 'You see,' he said. But that was as far as he got with what he was going to say, because at that moment the ground began to shake and the trees to rustle, and from behind them, not very far away, came the noise that was wolf or dragon, the loudest they had ever heard it, shouting at them; and if it was a dragon they could smell its breath, and see the cloudiness of it. No one this time said there were five of them and could not be frightened. They were all frightened. They all ran, as close together as they could get, stumbling through the trees, downhill, away from the noise.

seventeen

After a time they were not running so fast. They were all puffing and breathing so loud now that no other noise could have been heard. Rodney thought that they were running more quietly, but it was because he could not hear his feet, with Northman on one side sucking and blowing air, and Maureen on the other sipping and barking with breathlessness.

'Stop,' said Armadine, but they hardly heard her. They began to stop when they had to, when there seemed to be no more air left to breathe in the whole wood.

They stopped and held on to trees, and looked round, all of them together, to see whether they were being followed. The wood was empty behind them.

'I'm all winded out,' said Maureen. 'I can't even speak.' She could speak most, though, and the others had to wait longer until they could make words come from their mouths. Northman was trying to catch his breath and touch his toes at the same time, and hold his side and look all round him.

'Stitch?' said Leo. Northman nodded, among all his other activities.

'We're lost,' said Armadine, sitting down at last and putting her hair out of her eyes. 'We don't know where we are.'

'There'll be an edge somewhere,' said Leo. 'We'll have to go to it.'

'We can't go back,' said Maureen.

'No,' said Rodney. 'I won't look for my aeroplane any more. It's lost itself, and that's that.'

'Let's go on,' said Leo, getting up before he had all his breath back. 'We might see it.'

They went on, walking now, and listening to either side. They were among trees, there was no track to follow, there was no way of telling which direction they were taking. Leo said they might be going back towards the noise. Armadine said they should follow the sun, but when they looked for it overhead they remembered that the day was cloudy, though it was not raining. There was not even a wind to steer by.

The wood began to change its nature. The trees grew less high, and they could see further. Rodney thought he might have been here before, but Leo said it was just the wood looking like the rest of itself.

They came out of the wood, on to a rough grassland that was just like the grassland behind the house where Grandfather lived. But it was not the same place. Beyond it there was no fence and no village. There was a hedge, and beyond the hedge there were fields.

'I didn't feel so lost when I was in the woods,' said Maureen. 'Now you've lost me, and I've lived here always, and I should know it. I bet you're tricking me, because you've been funny about something all day.'

'Not about that,' said Armadine. 'Not about that at all.'

'Never mind about that,' said Leo. 'We'll wait until we've found where we are.'

'That's all you will find,' said Armadine. Rodney thought she was going to quarrel again, but she did not say any more.

There was a noise. It was a noise they all knew and had heard many times. A bicycle bell tinged not far away. They went towards where the sound had come from, and found that beyond the hedge there was a road.

'We're still lost,' said Leo. 'But now we won't go round in a circle or never find ourselves again. We'll find a sign-post soon, and get back like that.'

They climbed through the hedge, and stood on the road, and felt very much more found at once. The cyclist had gone, and they never saw him. He had just rung his bell at a corner, at the right moment, and led them out of the wilderness.

The decided which way to go by throwing a coin into the air and letting it fall. It was Leo's coin. He asked Rodney to decide whether heads or tails should be left or right. Rodney decided. Leo threw the coin up. 'I can't spin them,' he said. The coin fell head up, and Rodney pointed the way he had decided.

They went round the bend in the road, and there, at

once, they saw something that was not a signpost, but just as good: a railway station, with its name painted up outside it, and on the platforms. Hetbury, it said, and repeated it on the lamps.

'Why,' said Maureen, 'that's the next station to Kenge. I've been here before in the train.' And she explained where the line went. Rodney said that he must have been through it plenty of times before.

'Well,' said Leo, 'I wonder if there's a train back to Kenge. I've got some money.'

'Leo, you mustn't, David,' said Armadine.

'I'm not going to walk back, Susan,' said Leo. 'I mean Armadine. You can if you like.'

'You couldn't,' said Maureen. 'The road goes all round the common. It's a long way. And we don't want to walk back through the wood, do we?'

'All the same,' said Armadine. But she gave in. Rodney thought she was being awkward today and somehow against all the things Leo wanted to do.

They walked into the station, and stood in the archway that led to the platform. There was a little rumbling rattle, and a shutter flew up in the wall, and there was a man ready to sell tickets. Leo asked whether they could get to Kenge, and how long it was before there was a train.

The man said there was one due in half an hour, and that five halves would be ten pence each. Leo looked at Armadine, put his hand in his pocket, brought out a 50 pence piece, and handed it over. He was given five tickets in exchange, and they were told to go through on to the platform and not lark about.

'You've done it now,' said Armadine.

'I know,' said Leo. 'But we can't walk back, can we? There isn't much left.'

'Tell him,' said Armadine.

'Tell him,' said Northman.

'It's my money,' said Leo, looking at Rodney. 'And I lost your aeroplane, so I'm going to give you the money so you can get another. It was my fault, you see, wasn't it? I've been meaning to give it to you all day, but I thought we might find it, but we didn't, and we only got lost, and here's what's left, it's only 50 pence, but I'll save up the rest.'

eighteen

Leo held out the coin. Rodney looked at it. He didn't want it. He wanted the aeroplane, but he did not blame Leo for losing it. He might have flown it himself and lost it just as easily. He did not know how to refuse the money. Maureen helped him.

'You don't know about that aeroplane,' she told Leo. 'He never made it or got it given, or anything like that. It was lost before he got it.'

'Maureen knows where it came from,' said Rodney.

'I don't,' said Maureen. 'I just said that. But it wasn't worth anything, was it, Rodney?'

'Nothing,' said Rodney. 'Only its aeroplaneness.'

'You've got to have it,' said Leo, and since Rodney would not put out a hand for it he laid the coin on a station seat and walked away.

'He's always going back on his promises,' said Armadine. 'And he swore he would give it all to you. He's good sometimes, but it doesn't last until it gets there.'

Rodney sat next to the money. At the other end of the platform Leo examined the signals and a pair of points. He was leaning against the signal when it moved. They all heard it, because it was the only sound to be heard in the still dull afternoon.

Then the train could be heard, humming along the line, and then they could see it, not looking as if it were coming nearer, but seeming to stand in the same place and get bigger. They stood up, and the train drew right up to them and made a wall at the edge of the platform, and then slowed until there were doors and windows in the wall.

Leo waved to them to come to his end of the train, which was the front. They ran to him, leaving the coin behind. Maureen hesitated, then picked it up and dropped it into her jacket pocket.

It was a diesel train, and behind the driver's compartment was a whole empty division of the train, with a good forward view. They opened the door and got in. The driver heard them through the glass, and turned round and nodded.

A bell rang. The driver pulled gently at levers, and the train began to move.

'Why isn't he steering?' said Northman, looking with great anxiety at the driver.

There was a wheel like a steering-wheel beside the driver, but he was not using it. Leo tapped on the glass, and pointed to the wheel and made steering movements with his hands. The driver reached behind him and slid the door open.

'It's a handbrake,' he said. 'We run on rails. Most of the time.' He attended to his driving as he spoke, and pressed a button that blew a horn. 'Tunnel,' he said.

The land at the side of the line rose up like walls, and closed in the sky. There was an archway in front, looking quite black, with the lines vanishing into it. The train went out of daylight, blew its horn again, and lumbered through the tunnel.

There was nothing to see. There was only darkness.

Then, far ahead, there was a gleam of light. Leo said it was the end of the tunnel. The driver said it wasn't. 'A ventilation shaft,' he said, and slowed the train down even more. 'Look up,' he said. 'You can come in here.'

They all went into the driver's cab, and looked upwards out of the front windows. In the roof of the tunnel there was a round opening, with light coming down it and shining all round.

'Stop,' said Leo suddenly. 'Stop, driver, stop, stop, stop.'

'No nonsense,' said the driver making the train speed up a bit. 'You shouldn't be in here by rights.'

Leo was pointing ahead. 'Look,' he said, 'Look, there it is. The aeroplane, the aeroplane.'

'Leo,' said Armadine. 'Don't be silly.' But they all saw when they looked. The orange-striped aeroplane was sitting between the rails, in the light from the ventilation shaft and was quite plainly to be seen.

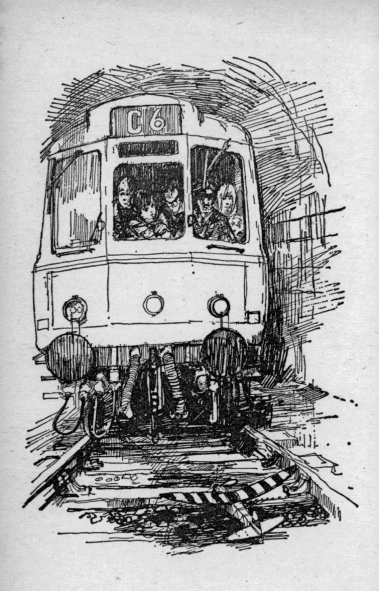

'It's mine,' said Rodney. 'It is.'

There was a hissing noise, and the train stopped, with the light of the shaft falling down into the cab.

'No, get back in and sit down,' said the driver. 'And I'll do you a favour. Don't know why.'

They all went back and sat down. The driver opened his door, and dropped down on to the track. He was back in a moment with the aeroplane. He put it on the brake wheel that looked like a steering-wheel, and started the train moving again. The light from the shaft vanished, and there was only darkness. The driver had switched off the carriage lamps so that they could see the tunnel better.

He slid the door between the compartments open again. 'What else have you dropped down?' he said.

'We haven't dropped anything anywhere,' said Rodney, because he was the one being spoken to. 'The aeroplane flew away and got lost in the woods.'

'There's a vent tower up on the common,' said the driver. 'Should be too tall for you to get into.'

'A tower?' said Leo. 'Just a tower without any doors or windows, made of stone?'

'Yes,' said the driver. 'Look, there's the end of the tunnel ahead. Just a tower. You can hear the trains going by underneath, not very far down, but a longish tunnel. They had to tunnel. Couldn't dig the common out, seemingly. Long tunnel has to have a vent. Your aeroplane flew down it.'

'And we often heard the noise,' said Leo.

'Felt it, too, I know,' said the driver. 'Used to go that way nutting when I was a lad, and the place would shake and smoke and roar with the big steam expresses.'

The train came out of the tunnel, and there was Kenge station ahead. The train stopped. The driver handed the aeroplane to Rodney. 'Needn't say how you came to find it,' he said. 'Don't put it down there again, that's all.'

'Thank you,' said Rodney.

'I hope you didn't leave my money at the station,' said Leo. But Maureen put her hand in her pocket and gave him the money back as they climbed out on to the platform. 'We'll listen for you tomorrow, blowing your horn,' said Leo, through the window to the engine driver. 'If it isn't raining.'

'Don't fall down it,' said the driver. 'I shan't stop to give you a lift.'

nineteen

Rodney was late for tea. Granny said she didn't know what he was coming to. Grandfather said that one day he would come back to find nothing had been left for him at all. Granny said Grandfather would do better to go and do some gardening.

Mother wanted to know why he looked so battered and hot and dirty. Rodney didn't know he did, but Mother said he was all those things. His clothes looked as if he had been fighting, and was it that Maureen Garley? Rodney said it wasn't, and Maureen was all right, and all she wanted was friends. And he had been hot once, running about in the wood, and he had probably got dirty in the woods too, or it might have been in the train.

Mother wanted to know at once all about the train, and what on earth had he been doing on it, and what did he mean by it?

Rodney explained. Granny said he was explaining backwards again, but she was so interested to know that she let him eat and talk at the same time, or very nearly the same time: he hadn't to have words and food in his mouth at the same time. She said he had to spit one or the other out. Mother said Granny hadn't to teach the boy such things, and Granny said, well, who had brought Mother up, then?

Mother said, when she had heard everything, that Rodney must give Leo the money for the train fare. Not Rodney's money, she said, but some she would provide. She gave him a coin from her handbag. When he got it it smelled of scent, but later in the evening it had lost the scent and had no smell at all.

There were Five Bad Eggs now, Leo said the next morning, when they all met at the Nest. He thought Maureen should be a real Bad Egg, and Rodney too, not just visiting ones. Then the tree shook, and the thing in the woods roared, and the smell that was the smell of insides of tunnels came through the trees.

'It's not the same,' said Leo. 'I quite like being frightened a little bit. But I didn't like it when I was frightened a lot. We should have stayed in this tree.'

They stayed in the tree all that morning, having races up and down it, and trying to do something about the door of the Nest, which had started opening inwards instead of outwards. It was very awkward if it would only open inwards when they were all in it, because there was no room for a door as well.

The aeroplane stayed safely at home. Rodney thought it might be getting tired, and it had certainly got rather dirty, with a sort of blackness that would not come off. And there was a small tear in the fabric of one wing. Otherwise it was in good health.

In the afternoon, after trying to lock the Nest up, and having to nail the door in the end, with the garden hammer and a spare nail, they went to the tower.

'I'm still a bit creepish about it,' said Armadine. 'What if the driver was talking about another tower? What time is he coming?'

'I looked at my watch,' said Leo. 'It was half past four when we got to Kenge station, so he'll get here just before then. It's quarter to four now.'

They all looked at the tower. It was Rodney who had the idea of climbing up a nearby tree and looking at the top of it, to see whether it was hollow. 'But it must be,' he said. 'Don't you think we ought to get ready to run again?'

'Run the other way this time,' said Leo. 'That's all.'

At about ten to four the ground shook, and the tower roared. Rodney was up in a tree by then, and looking down at the black mouth of the tower.

'Darkness comes up it,' he said. 'Light goes down, and dark comes up.' He spoke to the others, but when he looked they were not to be seen. Rodney came down from the tree and looked about. It was one of Leo's jokes, and they had hidden from him to scare him, and came out from the other side of the tower at once.

The hands of Leo's watch came slowly round towards half past four. There was no sign of a train yet. And then, when they thought it must be too late, it came, with the

ground shaking gently, because the diesel train was small and light and only moving slowly, not like the big expresses. Noise came up the tower and spilled over the top, noise of wheels and motors, and then a great big laugh of hornblowing, getting louder and louder, and then fainter and fainter.

'It is it,' said Leo. 'So we're quite safe here.'

'Tame wolf, tame dragon,' said Armadine.

'Tame engine driver,' said Rodney.

'Tame aeroplane,' said Maureen.

'Tame Maureen Garley,' said Northman, and closed his mouth and looked at the ground.

Elizabeth Clark
Stories to Tell 50p

Here are eight of Elizabeth Clark's finest stories, enchanting tales
for younger readers. With their country settings and magical themes
they are ideal for reading aloud as bedtime stories or by the
fireside on wet afternoons. Extra large type makes them just as
perfect for children to read for themselves.

Ann Lawrence
The Conjuror's Box 50p

It is just an ordinary old green jug with a white cat on the handle;
until, one afternoon, the white cat comes to life, introduces himself
as Snowy and takes Martin and Lucy into a magical adventure,
where they meet the mysterious and evil Green Lady, two striped
mice, a flying rocking-horse and the conjuror's box, the link with
a strange, new world.

retold by Amabel Williams-Ellis
Grimm's Fairy Tales   50p
More Grimm's Fairy Tales 45p

Here are two collections of some of the most famous Grimm
stories, such as 'Snow White and the Seven Dwarfs', 'The
Goose Girl', 'The Wolf and the Seven Little Kids', 'Mrs Owl' and
many others, all brought up to date and beautifully told and
Illustrated.

Henry Treece
The Bronze Sword 50p

All his life Drucus had been a soldier in the ranks of Caesar's
legions. But now the old centurion had settled down to the quiet
life of a farmer in the distant land of Britain under the rule of Rome.
Suddenly, the years of the sword had returned. Boudicca and her
fierce tribesmen had come to raid and pillage. The young warrior
with the bronze sword brings him the Queen's verdict on whether
he is to live or die ...

Rosemary Sutcliffe
The Chief's Daughter 50p

Long, long ago, the fierce Irish sea-raiders crossed the water to
ravage and plunder the coast of Wales. It was on one of these
raids that Welsh tribesmen captured Dara, the boy warrior, and
now the tribe's priest demands that he be killed. Dara must die as a
sacrifice to the great black goddess whose anger has made the
springs run dry. His only hope is Nellan, the chief's daughter, who
will even defy her father to save Dara's life ...